SPECKLED EGG FARM

Once upon a time on Speckled Egg Farm,
On top of the hill stood an old wooden barn,
The moon was full and the stars shone bright,
With everyone safely tucked up for the night.

All were excited and just couldn't rest,
Watching Mrs Chicken on top of her nest,
Warming four eggs on her little hay patch,
Patiently waiting for her chicks to hatch.

Suddenly, Mrs Chicken dropped her book!
Jumping off her nest as the little eggs shook,
With a wiggle and jiggle the chicks broke free,
All yellow and fluffy and cute as can be!

Then the last egg cracked,
but didn't quite break.
"Something's not right,
could it be a mistake?"

Through the hole in the egg,
something popped into sight,
Not fluffy and yellow...
BUT ALL
BLACK AND WHITE!

The animals moved closer,
so they could all see,
and gathering 'round said
**"WHAT COULD IT BE?"**
"Calm down" said Pig, "No need to stress,
What's in the egg, let's all take a guess!"

So Rooster went first "I do like a quiz!
From peeping inside I know what it is,
I've seen those birds swoop up in the sky,
your black and white chick is a huge..."

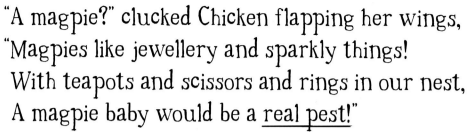

"A magpie?" clucked Chicken flapping her wings,
"Magpies like jewellery and sparkly things!
With teapots and scissors and rings in our nest,
A magpie baby would be a <u>real pest!</u>"

The Pig shuffled closer to have a good sniff,
"Phew! what a smell, it's a terrible whiff!
There's no need to worry about clutter and junk
Because inside this egg is a black and white..."

They all laughed at Pig...
"I don't think he knows!
That 'pong' is the mud on the end of your nose!"
Mrs Chicken was calm
as she peered in the shell,
"Thank goodness", she thought
"My baby won't smell!"

"It's no magpie or skunk!"
said the Duck with a smile.
"It's a bird like me, but a different style!
We don't look alike and he's not my twin,
But inside this egg is a fat..."

"A penguin!" cried Chicken, "Please tell me it's lies!"
And the tears filled up in her watery eyes.
"Penguins love skiing and freezing cold ice,
You'll need lots of woollies – if you take my advice!"

"Nonsense!" laughed Cat as he licked his paw,
"I know what's inside, it's the answer for sure!
I've been to the harbour and heard fishermen talk
Don't listen Chicken – this may make you squawk!"

"It's no magpie or skunk or cold penguin bird,
These guesses are silly and really absurd!"
"It's simple" smiled Cat, as he stroked his long tail,
"Inside this egg is a black and white..."

..."whale!"

"A WHALE!" gasped Chicken, "Oh, golly gosh!
A baby that big would be too hard to wash!
It would take me all day just to give him a scrub,
And how would it fit in our little bathtub?"

Dog laughed at the cat, "You silly old clot!
A magpie, skunk, penguin or whale it's not!
The answer's as easy as falling off a log..."

"Mrs Chicken's new baby is a..."

..."dalmatian dog!"

"But dogs love bones and chasing big sticks,
They've got soggy noses and slobbery licks,
How would we train it and teach it to run?
A big baby dog is simply no fun!"

The Goat crept closer to study the egg,
"It's not a dog, they're all pulling your leg!
Let's finish this game and get off to sleep,
this black and white thing is a big fluffy..."

..."sheep!"

Mrs Sheep stepped up and tried to take stock,
"It's not a breed I've seen in any farm flock",
On closer inspection she spotted a clue,
Then the penny just dropped – and she suddenly knew!

"It's not a magpie or skunk,
no penguin or whale,
Not a dog or a sheep
with a long wooly tail,
Just take a look closely,
This baby has hair..."

"Inside this egg is a large..."

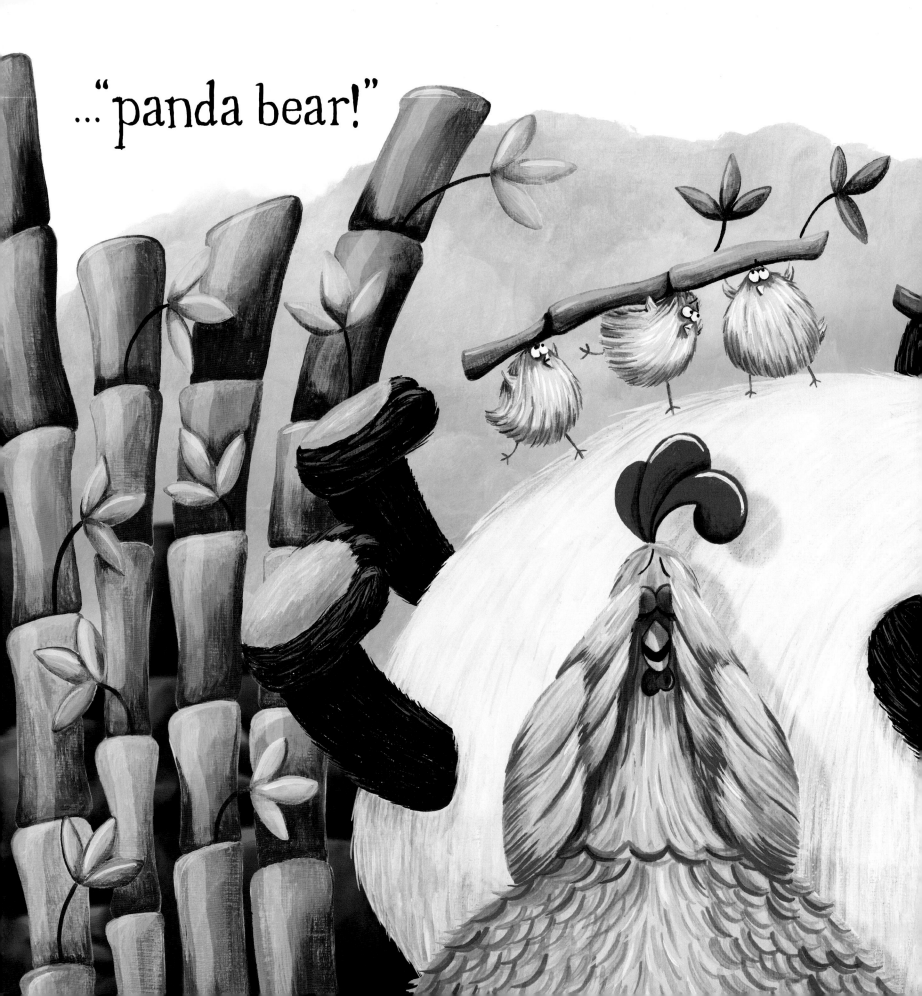

"A panda!" cried Chicken, "Don't say that it's true,
I'm not eating leaves and sticks of bamboo!
It's a calamity and really unfair...
How can we cope with a ginormous bear?"

Then Rabbit (who was sitting
in a small wooden box),
remembered a friend of old Mr Fox,
A bit like a bear,
he was black with some white,
Who sleeps in the day and
comes out at night.

"I've got it!" said Rabbit,
"I hope you'll eat SLUG!"
"Your baby, Mrs Chicken is a small..."

..."badger cub!"

"DISGUSTING!" said Chicken, "I'm not eating SLUG!
Or squeezing down tunnels my baby has dug!"
She pulled a sad face and then started to frown,
"How can I live in a hole underground?"

"These guesses are stupid (you know that of course!)"
Said the boastful and bragging, young Mr Horse.
He trotted on over and peered through the crack,
and spotted some stripes of white and then black.

"Unless I'm mistaken,
and let's face it I'm not!
This baby looks 'horsey'
And ready to trot!"
Like a donkey but fancy,
Like my cousin Deborah...

Congratulations Chicken,
You're having a..."

"A zebra!" screamed Chicken!
"But they live on the plains!
With big scary lions with long furry manes,
Living with zebra would sure make us thinner,
Running away so we're not someone's dinner!"

"Calm down!" said the Bull,
as he picked up the nest,
"Nobody's dining on our
chicken breast!
It's no magpie or skunk,
Nor penguin or whale,
Not a sheep or a dog with
a long waggy tail."

"It's not a panda or badger,
or daft stripy horse,
The answer's here on the
farm of course!"

"I'm not sure why,
or even know how,
But here in this egg
lives a black and white..."

..."A cow!" cried Chicken,

"What are we to do?
Just imagine the mud and smelly cow poo!"
So Mrs Chicken sat down and gave a big sigh.
And the three baby chicks all started to cry!

So they'd all had a turn,
And each had their guess.
The chicks were all crying,
Mrs Chicken was stressed.
The puzzle was over,
So what to do now?...

Poor Mrs Chicken
was having a cow!

In all the excitement and through the uproar,
the egg started wiggling and jiggling once more,

They all stepped back from the little hay patch
as they waited to see – a baby cow hatch!

Then, with a CRACK, the wiggling stopped,
the egg shell broke and out of it popped...

CRACK!

CRACK!

# A cute baby chick!

He wasn't yellow like the others, But that didn't matter now,
He was beautiful and different, (and he wasn't a cow!)

"Aaaahhhhh!"

The chicks gathered 'round as happy as can be,
To welcome the baby to the whole family!
Mummy then said "Let's have a good cuddle!"
And she scooped them all up
for a big chicken huddle!

With the excitement all over, then Mr Horse said...
"Let's all settle down, it's now time for bed!"

"MOOOO-VE OVER Mummy Chicken!"
Joked tired Mrs Sheep,
and they all laughed out loud
before falling asleep!

THE END

# If you enjoyed this book by Adam Bestwick you'll enjoy these too!...

*"My Dad's a great inventor, and he's building a machine,*
*It's a kind of housework robot, to keep my bedroom clean."*

When a new mechanical friend joins the family to help around the house, Robbie is impressed just how useful he is – cooking, sweeping, doing the dishes and tidying his room.

But instead of housework, Robbie has his own plans for the robot which could get him into a whole lot of trouble! Can anyone make the robot stop? A tale of nuts, bolts and mechanical mayhem!

*"When Ruby was a baby, Dad made a big mistake,*
*He gave her the wrong bottle when he wasn't quite awake,*
*From that day on it all went wrong, and nothing passed her lip*
*Without a generous topping of, Ruby's favourite dip!"*

A simple mistake from Dad has disastrous consequences in this fun, playful book that escalates more and more with each page! From emptying the local corner shop and growing their own crop, to the world's armed forces being drafted in, Ruby's family try in vain but can anyone quench her insatiable appetite for Ketchup? Inspired by his own kids' love for red sauce, this entertaining rhyming story will strike a chord with lots of families, down to the final twist in the tale!